Grumpy Bear

Best Friend Bear

W9-BPM-556

Secret Bear

This book belongs to:

Wish Bear

Love-a-lot Bear

No part of this publication may be reproduced in whole or in part, or stored in a retrieval system, or transmitted in any form or by any means, electronic, mechanical, photocopying, recording, or otherwise, without written permission of the publisher. For information regarding permission, write to: Scholastic Inc., Attention: Permissions Department, 557 Broadway, New York, NY 10012.

Published by Scholastic Inc.
90 Old Sherman Turnpike, Danbury, CT 06816.

SCHOLASTIC and associated logos are trademarks and/or registered trademarks of Scholastic Inc.

ISBN 0-439-79991-0

First Scholastic Printing, December 2005

Care Bears™
Friendship Club
Sleep Tight

by
Quinlan B. Lee

Illustrated by
Saxton Moore

SCHOLASTIC INC.

New York   Toronto   London   Auckland   Sydney
Mexico City   New Delhi   Hong Kong   Buenos Aires

The sun was going down in Care-a-lot, and most of the Care Bears were going to bed. Not Bedtime Bear. He was just getting up.

"Time to go to work," he said.

"Sweet dreams, everyone," Bedtime Bear whispered, winking at the moon.

Soon the only sounds
he heard were snores.

But then very softly, Bedtime Bear heard someone
crying. "Uh-oh, I think I know who that is," he said.

Bedtime Bear hurried to Best Friend Bear's bed.
"I'm afraid," Best Friend Bear said.

Bedtime Bear hugged her and said, "Best Friend Bear, there's no reason to be afraid. I'm just a cloud away, and I'll be watching over you."

"I know," she sighed. "But if only it weren't so dark."

He reached down and put some stars
on a cloud beside Best Friend Bear's bed.
"A night-light!" Best Friend Bear said. "Thank you!"

Bedtime Bear went back to his favorite
cloud and started counting stars. Suddenly
he heard someone calling him.

"Bedtime Bear!
Bedtime Bear,
come quickly!"

Bedtime Bear jumped off
his cloud and ran to see what
was happening.

He found Funshine Bear and Love-a-lot Bear
shaking in their beds.
"There's something behind that cloud,"
said Funshine Bear. "And it isn't funny!"

"It's something **big**," cried Love-a-lot Bear. "Look at its ears! I think it's something scary," she added.

"I think I will go see what it is," said Bedtime Bear bravely,

Bedtime Bear walked to the cloud
and peered around it.

Funshine Bear and Love-a-lot Bear
saw the shadow move toward them.

"Watch out!"
Funshine Bear cried.
    "Here it comes," said
Love-a-lot Bear. "It's a big . . .
it's a really big . . ."

"Balloon!" finished Bedtime Bear.
"I can't believe it," said Love-a-lot Bear, laughing.
"It looked so scary over there!"

"A lot of things can look scary that aren't," Bedtime Bear told them. "Sometimes it takes a friend to help you see things as they really are."

"You're right," said Funshine Bear. "Thanks, Bedtime Bear."

When morning came,
the Care Bears stretched
and got out of their beds.

22

But not Bedtime Bear. He stretched and crawled *into* his bed.

"It's past my bedtime," he said, yawning.

Later that morning, Wish Bear tried to wake
up Bedtime Bear to go roller-skating. But Bedtime
Bear only yawned and rolled over on his cloud.

In the afternoon, Secret Bear and Share Bear wanted Bedtime Bear to help plant a garden. But he kept on napping.

While the sun was setting and the shadows grew long,
Bedtime Bear finally woke up.

He rubbed his eyes and looked around for his friends. Bedtime Bear didn't see them. But behind a cloud, he saw something big and . . .

SCARY!

"Look over there," Bedtime Bear called, pointing at a dark shadow. "What's that?"

"I don't know," said Love-a-lot Bear.
"And I don't think I want to know."

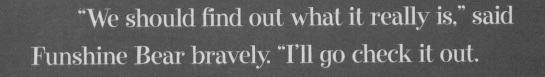

"We should find out what it really is," said Funshine Bear bravely. "I'll go check it out.

Who will go with me?"

Best Friend Bear suddenly stood up tall. "I will," she said.

29

The two Care Bears came back in no time.
"It was something scary," said Best Friend Bear.
"A scary-crow from Secret's garden."

Bedtime Bear blushed. "A scarecrow isn't scary. I shouldn't have been afraid. I'm supposed to be brave."

"Being brave doesn't mean you're never scared," said Love-a-lot Bear. "It means you keep going even when you're afraid."

Funshine Bear added, "Remember, sometimes it takes a friend to help you see things as they really are.'"

"And you really are the bravest Care Bear of all," said Best Friend Bear.

"Thank you," said Bedtime Bear. "But it's getting dark, and you know what that means."

"Time for the stars to shine!" said Best Friend Bear.
"You're right," Bedtime Bear chuckled. "There's one more thing that shines best when you're in the dark."

"What?" said Best Friend Bear, snuggling into bed.
"True friends," whispered Bedtime Bear.

"Just like all of you."

How Can You Be Brave Like Bedtime Bear?

Best Friend Bear was afraid of the dark,
but a night-light made her feel better.

💜 Is there anything you are afraid of?

💜 What makes you feel less afraid?

36

Funshine Bear, Love-a-lot Bear, and even Bedtime Bear thought something was scary that really wasn't.

♥ Has that ever happened to you?

♥ How did you find out that it wasn't really something scary?

Funshine Bear and Love-a-lot Bear learned to be brave like Bedtime Bear.

♥ When have you done something brave?

♥ Have you ever helped a friend by being brave?

Bashful Heart Bear

Cheer Bear

Share Bear

Bedtime Bear

Funshine Bear